melville house classics

THE HORLA

THE HORLA

GUY DE MAUPASSANT

TRANSLATED BY CHARLOTTE MANDELL

 MELVILLE HOUSE PUBLISHING
BROOKLYN, NEW YORK

"LETTER FROM A MADMAN" WAS FIRST PUBLISHED IN 1885.
THE FIRST VERSION OF "THE HORLA" WAS PUBLISHED IN 1886;
THE FINAL VERSION WAS PUBLISHED IN 1887.

TRANSLATION © 2005 CHARLOTTE MANDELL
BOOK DESIGN: DAVID KONOPKA

MELVILLE HOUSE PUBLISHING
145 PLYMOUTH STREET
BROOKLYN, NY 11201

WWW.MHPBOOKS.COM

3 4 5 6 7 8 9 10

ISBN: 0-9761407-4-8

LIBRARY OF CONGRESS CATALOGING-IN-PUBLICATION DATA

Maupassant, Guy de, 1850–1893.
    [Horla. English]
    The horla / Guy de Maupassant ; translated by Charlotte Mandell.
        p. cm.
    ISBN 0-9761407-4-8
    i. Mandell, Charlotte. II. Title.
    PQ2349.H713 2005
    843'.8—dc22

2005010708

TABLE OF CONTENTS

THE HORLA

May 8. What a wonderful day! I spent all morning stretched out on the grass in front of my house, beneath the huge plane tree that completely covers, shelters, and shades the lawn. I love the country here, and I love living here because this is where I have my roots, those profound and delicate roots that attach a man to the land where his ancestors were born and died, and that attach him to what one should think and what one should eat; to customs as well as to foods; to local idioms and peasant intonations; to the smells of the earth, of the villages, of the air itself.

I love my house, I grew up in it. From my windows, I can see the Seine flowing along the whole length of my garden, behind the road, almost in my back yard, the great, wide Seine, which goes from Rouen to Le Havre, covered with boats passing by.

To the left, over there, Rouen, the vast blue-roofed city, beneath the peaked crowd of Gothic bell towers. They are countless, slender or broad, dominated by the iron spire of the cathedral, and full of bells that ring in the blue air on fine mornings, carrying towards me their gentle, distant metal drone, their bronze song the breeze carries to me, now stronger, now weaker, depending on whether the wind is awakening or growing drowsy.

How fine it was this morning!

Around eleven o'clock, a long procession of ships, pulled by a tugboat fat as a fly, groaning from the effort and vomiting a thick plume of smoke, filed past my gate.

After two English schooners, whose red flags rippled on the sky, came a superb Brazilian three-master, all white, admirably clean and gleaming. I saluted it, I don't know why, it made me so happy to see this ship.

May 11. I've been a little feverish for a few days now. I feel unwell, or rather I feel sad.

Where do these mysterious influences come from that change our happiness into despondency and our confidence into distress? You might say that the air, the invisible air, is full of unknowable Powers, from whose mysterious closeness we suffer. I wake up full of joy, with songs welling up in my throat. Why? I go down to the water; and suddenly, after a short walk, I come back disheartened, as if some misfortune were awaiting me at home. Why? Is it a shiver of cold that, brushing against my skin, has affected my nerves and darkened my soul? Is it the shape of the clouds, or the color of the daylight, the color of things, so changeable, that, passing in front of my eyes, has disturbed my thoughts? How can we know? Everything that surrounds us, everything we see without looking at it, everything we brush against without recognizing it, everything we touch without feeling it, everything we encounter without discerning it, everything has on us, on our organs, and, through them, on our ideas, on our heart itself, swift, surprising, and inexplicable effects.

How profound this mystery of the Invisible is! We cannot fathom it with our wretched senses, with our eyes that don't know how to perceive either the too-small or the too-big, the too-close or the too-far, the inhabitants of a star or the inhabitants of a drop of water... with our ears that deceive us, for they transmit to us the vibrations of the air as ringing tones. They are fairies that perform the miracle of changing this movement into a sound, and by this metamorphosis, give birth to music, which makes the mute agitation of nature into a song... with our sense of smell, weaker than a dog's... with our sense of taste, which can scarcely tell the age of a wine.

If only we had other organs that could work other miracles for us, how many things we could then discover around us!

May 16. I am sick, no doubt about it—and I was feeling so healthy last month! I have a fever, a terrible fever, or rather a feverish nervous exhaustion, which makes my soul as sick as my body. I keep having this terrifying feeling of some danger threatening, this apprehension of a misfortune on the way, or of death approaching, this premonition that must be the onset of a sickness still unknown, germinating in the blood and the flesh.

May 18. I've just gone to consult my doctor, since I could no longer sleep. He found my pulse was rapid, my eyes dilated, my nerves vibrating, but without any alarming symptom. I must submit to taking showers and drinking potassium bromide.

May 25. No change. Really, I am in a strange condition. As evening approaches, an incomprehensible anxiety invades me, as if night hid a terrible threat for me. I dine quickly, then I try to read; but I do not understand the words. I can scarcely make out the letters. Then I walk back and forth in my living room, under the oppression of a confused and irresistible fear, the fear of sleep and fear of my bed.

Around ten o'clock, I climb up to my bedroom. As soon as I'm inside, I turn the key twice and bolt the locks; I am afraid... of what?... I never feared anything till now.... I open my wardrobes, look under my bed, listen... listen... for what? Is it strange that a simple illness, a circulatory disorder perhaps, an irritated nerve ending, a little congestion, a tiny perturbation in the all too imperfect and delicate functioning of our living mechanism, can turn the happiest of men into a melancholic, and the bravest into a coward? Then I go to bed, and I wait for sleep like someone waiting for the executioner. I wait for it, with terror at its arrival; and my heart beats, my legs tremble; and my whole body trembles in the warmth of the bedclothes, till the moment I suddenly fall into repose, the way one drowns oneself, dropping into an abyss of stagnant water. I don't feel it coming, as I used to, this treacherous sleep, hidden beside me, that lies in wait for me, that is about to seize me by the head, close my eyes, annihilate me.

I sleep—for a long time—two or three hours— then a dream—no—a nightmare grips me. I am fully aware that I am lying down and sleeping.... I feel it and I know it... and I also feel that someone is approaching me, looking at me, feeling me, is climbing into my bed, kneeling on my chest, taking my neck in his hands and squeezing... squeezing... with all his strength, to strangle me.

And I struggle with myself, bound by the atrocious powerlessness that paralyzes us in dreams. I want to cry out—I cannot. I want to move—I cannot. I try, with terrible efforts, gasping for breath, to turn over, to throw off this being that is crushing me and suffocating me—I can't!

And all of a sudden, I wake up, panic-stricken, covered with sweat. I light a candle. I am alone.

After this crisis, which is renewed every night, I finally sleep, calmly, until dawn.

June 2. My condition has become even worse. What do I have? The bromide does nothing for it; the showers do nothing. This afternoon, in order to tire out my body (which was weary to begin with), I went to the forest of Roumare for a walk. First I thought that the fresh air, gentle and sweet, full of the fragrance of grass and leaves, would imbue my veins with a new blood, my heart with a new energy. I took a broad avenue we use for hunting, then turned towards La Bouille by a narrow path between two armies of unusually tall trees that set a thick, green, almost black roof between the sky and me.

Suddenly I was seized by a shiver, but not of cold—a strange shiver of anxiety.

I quickened my step, uneasy at being alone in this wood, frightened for no reason, stupidly, because of the profound solitude. All of a sudden, it seemed to me I was being followed, that someone was walking just behind me, very close, very close, close enough to touch me.

I turned around suddenly. I was alone. Behind me I saw only the straight, wide lane, empty, high, terribly empty; and in the other direction it also stretched away out of sight, exactly the same, terrifying.

I closed my eyes. Why? And I began to spin on one heel, very quickly, like a top. I almost fell; I opened my eyes again; the trees were dancing; the earth was floating; I had to sit down. And then, I no longer knew how I had gotten there! Strange idea! Strange! Strange idea! I didn't know anymore. I left by the path that was at my right, and I returned to the avenue that had brought me to the middle of the forest.

June 3. The night was horrible. I am going to go away for a few weeks. A little journey will surely set me to rights.

July 2. I have returned. I am cured. And I've had a delightful excursion, too. I visited Mont Saint-Michel, which I'd never seen before.

What a vision, when you arrive, as I did, in Avranches, towards the end of day! The city is on a hill; and I was led into the public garden, on the edge of the city. I let out a cry of astonishment. A vast bay stretched out in front of me, as far as the eye could see, between two coasts far apart from each other, disappearing in the distance into the mist; and in the middle of this immense yellow bay, beneath a luminous golden sky, there rose up, dark and sharp-pointed, a strange mountain, in the middle of the sands. The sun had just disappeared, and on the still blazing horizon the outline of this fantastic rock stood out, bearing on its summit a fantastic monument.

At dawn, I went towards it. The sea was low, as it had been the night before, and I watched the surprising abbey rise before me as I approached it. After several hours of walking, I reached the massive hill of stones that supports the little city dominated by the great church. After climbing the narrow, steep street, I entered the most wonderful Gothic dwelling built for God on Earth, vast as a city, full of low chambers crushed beneath vaults, and high galleries supported by frail columns. I entered this giant granite jewel, light as lace, covered with towers and slim pinnacles, in which winding staircases rise up, and which hurl into the blue sky of day, and the dark sky of night, their strange heads bristling with chimeras, devils, fantastic animals, monstrous flowers, and which are linked to each other by slender, finely carved arches.

When I was at the summit, I said to the monk who was with me, "Father, how happy you must be here!"

He answered, "It is very windy, Monsieur"; and we set to talking as we watched the sea rise, as it came running onto the sand and covering it with a breastplate of steel.

And the monk told me stories, all the old stories of this place, legends, always more legends.

One of them particularly struck me. The local people, the ones who live on the hill, claim they hear voices at night in the sands. They say they hear two goats bleating, one with a strong voice, the other with a feeble voice. Scoffers assert they're the cries of seabirds, which sometimes resemble bleating, and sometimes human moans; but late-night fishermen swear they have seen, roaming about on the dunes, between the two tides, around the little town cast so far from the world, an old shepherd, whose head, covered with his cloak, could never be seen; and who led, walking in front of them, a billygoat with a man's face, and a nanny-goat with a woman's face, both with long white hair, talking ceaselessly, arguing with each other in an unknown language, then suddenly stopping to bleat with all their might.

I said to the monk, "Do you believe this?"

He murmured, "I don't know!"

I said, "If other beings besides us exist on Earth, why didn't we meet them a long time ago? Why haven't you yourself seen them? Why haven't I seen them, myself?"

He replied, "Do we see the hundred-thousandth part of what exists? Look, here is the wind, which is the strongest force in nature, which knocks men down, destroys buildings, uproots trees, whips the sea up into mountains of water, destroys cliffs, and throws great ships onto the shoals; here is the wind that kills, whistles, groans, howls—have you ever seen it, and can you see it? Yet it exists."

I fell silent before this simple reasoning. This man was a wise man, or perhaps an idiot. I wasn't able rightly to tell; but I fell silent. What he said then, I had often thought.

July 3. I slept badly; there must indeed be a feverish influence here, for my coachman suffers from the same illness as I do. When I returned yesterday, I noticed his unusual pallor. I asked him:

"What is wrong with you, Jean?"

"I can no longer rest, Monsieur; my nights are eating up my days. Since Monsieur left, that's what's been sticking to me like a curse."

The other servants are doing well, though, but I am very afraid of a relapse.

July 4. Without a doubt, I have caught it again. My old nightmares are coming back. Last night, I felt someone squatting over me, who, with his mouth over mine, was drinking in my life through my lips. Yes, he was sucking it in from my throat, just like a leech. Then he rose, sated, and I woke up, so wounded, broken, and annihilated, that I could no longer move. If that goes on for a few more days, I will definitely go away again.

July 5. Have I lost my reason? What I saw last night is so strange that my head spins when I think of it!

As I do now each evening, I had locked my door; then, since I was thirsty, I drank half a glass of water, and I noted by chance that my carafe was full to its crystal stopper.

Then I went to bed, and fell into one of my dreadful sleeps, from which I was snatched after about two hours by an even more frightful shock.

Imagine a man asleep, who is being killed, and who wakes up with a knife in his lung, with a death rattle, covered in blood, who can no longer breathe, who will die, and doesn't understand why—that's what it's like.

Having finally come to my senses, I was thirsty again; I lit a candle and went towards the table where my carafe was. I raised it and tipped it over my glass; nothing poured out.—It was empty! It was completely empty! First, I was at a complete loss; then, all of a sudden, I experienced such a terrible emotion that I had to sit down, or rather, fall into a chair. Then I bounded up again to look around me. Then I sat down again, overcome with astonishment and fear, before the transparent crystal! I contemplated it fixedly, trying to comprehend. My hands were trembling! Someone must have drunk this water. Who? Me? It must be me; it could only be me. So I was a sleepwalker, then, and was living, without knowing it, this double mysterious life, which makes us suspect that there are two beings inside us, or that a foreign being, unknowable and invisible, animates our captive body when our soul is dulled; and our body obeys this other being as it does ourselves, or obeys it more than ourselves.

Who can understand my abominable anguish? Who can understand the emotion of a man, of a healthy mind, wide awake, full of reason, who looks through the glass of a carafe, terrified that a little water has disappeared while he slept. And I stayed there till daylight, without daring to return to my bed.

July 6. I am going mad. Again someone drank the entire contents of my carafe last night—or rather, I drank it.

But is it me? Is it me? Who could it be? Who? Oh my God! am I going mad? Who can save me?

July 10. I have just carried out some surprising experiments.

Without a doubt, I am mad! And yet...

On July 6, before I went to bed, I placed on my table some wine, some milk, some water, some bread, and some strawberries.

Someone drank—I drank—all the water, and a little milk. They didn't touch the wine, or the bread, or the strawberries.

On July 7, I repeated the same test, which gave the same result.

On July 8, I didn't include the water and the milk. They touched nothing.

Finally, on July 9, I put on my table just the water and the milk, taking care to wrap the carafes in pieces of white muslin, and to tie down the stoppers. Then I rubbed my lips, beard, and hands with graphite, and I went to bed.

The invincible sleep seized me, followed soon after by the atrocious awakening. I had not moved at all; my covers themselves did not have any stains. I rushed over to my table. The pieces of cloth enclosing the bottles had remained spotless. I undid the strings, quivering with fear. Someone had drunk all the water! And all the milk! Oh my God...

I am going to leave soon for Paris.

July 12. Paris. I must have lost my head, those last few days. I must have been the plaything of my exhausted imagination, unless I am actually a sleep-walker, or have undergone one of those influences, which have been observed but are yet to be explained, that are called 'suggestive.' In any case, my panic was bordering on madness, but twenty-four hours in Paris have sufficed to restore my composure.

Yesterday, after I did some shopping and paid some visits, which made me enter into the mood of the fresh, invigorating air, I ended my evening at the Théâtre-Français. They were performing a play by Alexandre

Dumas the younger, and that alert, powerful wit completed my cure. Solitude is indeed dangerous for a working intelligence. We need to have around us people who think and speak. When we are alone for a long time, we people the void with phantoms.

I came back to the hotel very happy, by way of the boulevards. Rubbing shoulders with the crowd, I thought, not without irony, of my recent terrors and surmises, when I believed, yes, I believed an invisible being was living beneath my roof. How weak our head is, how easily alarmed it is, how quickly it wanders, as soon as a little incomprehensible fact strikes us!

Instead of concluding with these simple words: "I do not understand because the cause escapes me," we immediately imagine terrifying mysteries and supernatural powers.

July 14. Bastille Day. I walked about in the streets. I was as delighted by the firecrackers and flags as a child. It is idiotic, though, to be happy on schedule, on a day decreed by the government. The people are an imbecilic herd, sometimes stupidly patient and sometimes ferociously rebellious. They are told, "Have fun." They have fun. They are told, "Go fight with your neighbor." They go fight. They are told, "Vote for the Emperor." They vote for the Emperor. Then, they are told: "Vote for the Republic." And they vote for the Republic.

Those who run it are also fools; but instead of obeying people, they obey principles, which can only be inane, impotent, and false because of the very fact that they *are* principles, that is, ideas imagined to be definite and immutable, in this world where we are sure of nothing, since light is an illusion, since sound is an illusion.

July 16. I saw some things yesterday that troubled me very much.

I was dining at my cousin's, Madame Sablé, whose husband is in command of the 76th Chasseurs in Limoges. I was there as a guest along with two young women, one of whom had married a doctor, Dr. Parent, who spends much of his time studying nervous illnesses and the extraordinary symptoms that experiments with hypnotism and suggestion are producing these days.

He told us at great length about the incredible results obtained by English scholars and by doctors in the Nancy school.

The facts he mentioned seemed to me so bizarre that I told him I didn't believe him at all.

"We are," he asserted, "on the verge of discovering one of the most important secrets of nature, I mean one of its most important secrets on this earth, for nature must have far more important ones, up there, in the stars. Ever since man has thought, ever since he has known how to speak and write his thoughts, he has felt touched by a mystery impenetrable to his coarse and imperfect senses, and he has tried, by the effort of his intelligence, to compensate for the powerlessness of his organs. When this intelligence was still in its rudimentary state, this haunting by invisible phenomena took frightening forms of the most commonplace kind. Hence popular beliefs in the supernatural were born, legends of wandering spirits, fairies, gnomes, ghosts, I will even say the legend of God, for our concepts of the   artificer-creator, from whatever religion they come to us, are indeed the most mediocre inventions, the stupidest, the most unacceptable ones ever to have come from the frightened brains of creatures. Nothing is truer than this saying of Voltaire's: 'God made man in his image, but man has returned the favor.'

"But for a little more than century there has been a presentiment of something new. Mesmer and a few others have put us on an unexpected track, and we have truly arrived, especially in the last four or five years, at surprising results."

My cousin, also very skeptical, smiled. Dr. Parent said to her,

"Do you want me to try to put you to sleep, Madame?"

"Yes, I'd like that very much."

She sat down in an armchair and he began to look at her fixedly, hypnotizing her. I felt all of a sudden a little troubled; my heart was beating and my throat tightened. I saw Madame Sablé's eyes becoming heavier, her mouth clenching, her chest heaving.

After ten minutes, she was asleep.

"Position yourself behind her," the doctor said to me.

So I sat down behind her. He placed in her hands a visiting card and said to her, "This is a mirror. What do you see in it?"

She replied, "I see my cousin."

"What is he doing?"

"He is twisting his moustache."

"And now?"

"He is taking a photograph out of his pocket."

"What does this photograph show?"

"Himself."

It was true! And this photograph had just been delivered to me, that very evening, at the hotel.

"How is he shown in this portrait?"

"He is standing, with his hat in his hand."

So she could see in this card, in this white pasteboard, as she would have seen in a mirror.

The other young women, terrified, said, "That's enough! Enough! Enough!"

But the doctor commanded, "You will get up tomorrow at eight o'clock; then you will go find your cousin at his hotel, and you will beg him to lend you five thousand francs, which your husband asks you for, and which he needs to get from you for his next trip."

Then he woke her up.

As I was returning to the hotel, I thought about this curious séance, and I began to be assailed by doubts—not about the absolute, unquestionable good faith of my cousin, whom I have known like my sister, since childhood, but about the possible trickery of the doctor. Might he not have been hiding a mirror in his hand, which he was showing to the young woman asleep, at the same time as his visiting card? Professional magicians are known to do even more unusual things.

I returned, then, and went to bed.

This morning, around eight-thirty, I was awakened by my valet, who said to me:

"Madame Sablé is here, asking to speak to Monsieur right away."

I dressed myself in haste and invited her in.

She sat down, very agitated, her eyes lowered, and, without raising her veil, she said to me:

"My dear cousin, I have a great favor to ask you."

"What is it, cousin?"

"It embarrasses me very much to tell you, but I must. I am in need, in dire need, of five thousand francs."

"Really? You?"

"Yes, me, or rather, my husband, who has asked me to get them."

I was so stupefied that I stammered out my replies. I wondered if she and Dr. Parent weren't really making fun of me, if this weren't simply a farce prepared in advance and very well played.

But, as I looked at her attentively, all my doubts dissipated. She was trembling with anxiety, so painful was this task to her, and I could tell that her throat was choking with sobs.

I knew she was very wealthy, and I continued:

"But doesn't your husband have five thousand francs at his disposal? Think about it. Are you really sure he told you to ask me for them?"

She hesitated for a few seconds, as if she were making a great effort to search through her memory, then replied:

"Yes... yes... I am sure."

"He wrote to you?"

She hesitated again, thinking. I could see how hard it was for her to think. She didn't know. She just knew that she had to borrow five thousand francs from me for her husband. So she dared to lie.

"Yes, he wrote to me."

"When? You never mentioned it to me yesterday."

"I only received his letter this morning."

"Can you show it to me?"

"No... no... no... it contained private matters... too personal... I... I burned it."

"So, your husband has debts, then?"

She hesitated again, then murmured:

"I don't know."

I stated flatly: "The fact is, I can't give you five thousand francs right now, my dear cousin."

She let out a sort of cry of anguish.

"Oh! I implore you, I implore you, find them...."

She became distraught, joining her hands together as if she were praying to me! I heard her voice change tone. She cried and stammered, tormented, dominated by the irresistible order she had received.

"Oh! I beg you... if you only knew how much I am suffering... I must have the money today."

I took pity on her.

"You will have it this afternoon, I swear to you."

She cried out: "Oh! Thank you! Thank you! How good you are."

I continued: "Do you remember what happened yesterday at your house?"

"Yes."

"Do you remember that Dr. Parent put you to sleep?"

"Yes."

"Well, he ordered you to come to me this morning to borrow five thousand francs from me, and you are obeying his suggestion right now."

She thought for a few seconds and replied:

"But it's my husband who wants them."

I tried to convince her for an hour, but didn't succeed.

When she had left, I ran over to the doctor's. He was about to go out; and he listened to me, smiling. Then he said:

"Do you believe now?"

"Yes, I'm compelled to."

"Let's go to your cousin's."

She was already napping on a chaise longue, overwhelmed with fatigue. The doctor took her pulse, looked at her for some time, then raised his hand over her eyes. Gradually they closed, under the irresistible force of this magnetic power.

When she had fallen asleep:

"Your husband no longer needs the five thousand francs. You are going to forget that you begged your cousin to lend them to you. If he speaks to you about it, you will not understand."

Then he woke her up. I took my wallet out of my pocket.

"Here, dear cousin, is what you asked me for this morning."

She was so surprised that I didn't dare insist. I did try to revive her memory, but she strongly denied everything, thought I was making fun of her, and, in the end, almost became angry.

. . .

There you have it. I have just returned; I couldn't eat lunch, so upsetting this experience was for me.

July 19. Many people to whom I reported this adventure made fun of me. I no longer know what to think. The wise man says, "Perhaps!".

July 21. I went out to dine in Bougival; then I spent the evening at a dance at the rowing club. Decidedly, everything depends on places and environments. To believe in the supernatural on the Ile de la Grenouillère would be the height of folly... but on top of Mont Saint-Michel? Or in India? We are appallingly subject to the influence of our surroundings. I will return to my house next week.

July 30. I have been back home since yesterday. Everything is fine.

August 2. Nothing new; the weather is superb. I spend my days watching the Seine flow by.

August 4. Quarrels among the servants. They claim someone is breaking the glasses at night in the china closets. The valet blames the cook, who blames the laundress, who blames the other two. Who is guilty? Who can say, in the end?

August 6. This time, I am not mad. I saw... I saw... I saw! I can no longer doubt—I saw! I am still cold down to my fingertips... I am still afraid to the marrow of my bones... I saw!

I was taking a walk at two o'clock, in the full sunlight, in my rose garden... in the lane of autumn roses, which are beginning to flower.

As I was pausing to look at a *Géant des Batailles*, which bore three magnificent flowers, I saw, very distinctly, quite close to me, the stem of one of these roses bend itself, as if an invisible hand were twisting it, then break off, as if this hand had plucked it! Then the flower rose up, following the curve an arm would have described when carrying it toward a mouth, and it remained suspended in the transparent air, all alone, immobile, a terrifying red shape three feet from my eyes.

Agitated, I threw myself on it, to seize it. I found nothing; it had disappeared. Then I was overcome with a furious rage at myself; for a reasonable, serious man may not permit himself such hallucinations.

But was this truly a hallucination? I turned back to look for the stem, and I found it immediately on the shrub, freshly broken, between the two other roses that remained on the branch.

Then I returned to my house, my soul in turmoil; for I am certain, now, certain as I am of the alternation of day and night, that there exists close to me an invisible being, who feeds on milk and water, who can touch things, hold them, and make them change places. He is gifted, consequently, with a material nature, although it is imperceptible to our senses, and he is living, as I am, beneath my roof....

August 7. I slept calmly. It drank the water from my carafe, but did not trouble my sleep at all.

I wonder if I am crazy. As I was walking just now in the full sunshine, along the river, doubts about my reason came to me, not vague doubts as I have had till now, but precise, absolute doubts. I have seen madmen; I have known some who remained intelligent, lucid, even perceptive about all matters of life, except on one point. They speak of everything with clarity, agility, and profundity, and suddenly, as their thoughts turn to the stumbling-block of their madness, their thought processes shatter, scatter, and sink into that terrifying and furious ocean, full of leaping waves, fogs, and squalls, which we call "dementia".

Surely, I would think myself crazy, absolutely crazy, if I weren't aware of my condition, if I weren't completely familiar with it, if I didn't probe it by means of the most complete and lucid analysis. So I am in fact just a rational person suffering from hallucinations. An unknown distress has been produced in my brain, one of those distresses that the physiologists of today try to observe and explain. This distress has established a profound divide in my mind, in the order and logic of my ideas. Similar phenomena occur in dreams, which parade us through the most implausible phantasmagoria without our being surprised, since the verifying apparatus, the sense of control, is asleep, while the imaginative faculty is awake and at work. Isn't it possible that one of those imperceptible keys on the cerebral keyboard has become paralyzed in me? After an accident, people can lose their memory of proper names or verbs or numbers, or just dates. The localizations of all these fragments of thought have now been proven. So what is so surprising about the fact that my faculty of controlling the unreality of certain hallucinations has been numbed in me for the moment?

I was thinking about all of that as I followed the water's edge. The sun was coating the river with brightness, making the land delightful, filling my gaze with love for life, for the swallows, whose agility is a joy to my eyes, for the grasses on shore, whose rustling is a delight to my ears.

Little by little, however, an inexplicable uneasiness penetrated me. A force, it seemed to me, an occult force was making me go numb, stopping me, preventing me from going further, was calling me back. I felt that painful need to return that oppresses you when you have left an ailing loved one at home, and you suddenly feel a premonition that the sickness has grown worse.

So I returned, despite myself, certain that I was going to find, in my house, some piece of bad news, a letter or a telegram. There was nothing there, yet I was more surprised and anxious than if I had had another fantastic vision.

August 8. I had a frightful evening yesterday. It no longer manifests itself, but I feel it close to me, spying on me, watching me, penetrating me, dominating me, being all the more dreadful by hiding itself than if it gave some sign of its invisible and constant presence by means of supernatural phenomena.

Yet I slept.

August 9. Nothing, but I am afraid.

August 10. Nothing. What will happen tomorrow?

August 11. Still nothing. I can no longer remain at home with this fear and this thought always in my soul. I am going to go away.

August 12, 10 o'clock in the evening. All day I wanted to leave, but I could not. I wanted to perform this act of freedom that is so easy, so simple—going out—climbing into my carriage to go to Rouen—but I could not. Why?

August 13. When one is stricken with certain illnesses, all the resources of the physical being seem to be destroyed, all energies annihilated, all muscles limp. The bones seem to have become soft as flesh, and the flesh liquid as water. I am experiencing exactly that in my moral fiber in a strange and distressing way. I have lost all strength, all courage, all self-control, even all power to put my will in motion. I can no longer want anything; but someone wants for me; and I obey.

August 14. I am lost. Someone possesses my soul and governs it. Someone controls all my actions, all my movements, all my thoughts. I am nothing inside, nothing but a slave spectator, terrified of all the things I do. I want to go out. I cannot. It doesn't want to, so I remain, distraught, trembling, in the armchair where it is keeping me seated. I just want to get up, to stand up, just to believe I am still master of myself. I can't. I am riveted to my chair; my chair sticks to the floor, so that no strength can raise us.

Then all of a sudden, I must, I must go to the back of my garden to pick strawberries and eat them. And I go. I pick strawberries and I eat them! Oh my God! My God! Is there a God? If there is, set me free, save me! Help me! Forgive me! Have pity on me! Mercy! Save me! Save me from this suffering—this torture—this horror!

August 15. Surely this is how my poor cousin was possessed and dominated, when she came to borrow five thousand francs from me. She was undergoing a strange will that had entered her, like another soul, like a parasitic and dominating soul. Is the world about to end?

But the one that is governing me, what is it, this invisible thing? This unknowable thing, this prowler from a supernatural race?

So Invisible Beings do exist! But why haven't they ever revealed themselves in a clear way since the beginning of the world, as they are doing for me? I have never read anything that resembles what has been going on in my house. If only I could leave it, if only I could go out, flee and not come back, I would be saved. But I cannot.

August 16. I was able to escape today for two hours, like a prisoner who finds the door of his dungeon left open by chance. I felt I was free all of a sudden, and that he was far away. I ordered the carriage to be harnessed quickly, and I reached Rouen. What joy it was to be able to say to someone who obeys: "Go to Rouen!"

I had him stop in front of the library, and I asked them to lend me the great treatise by Dr. Hermann Herestauss on the unknown inhabitants of the ancient and modern world.

Then, as I was climbing back into my carriage, I wanted to say, "To the train station!" but I shouted— not said, but shouted—in such a loud voice that a passersby turned around, "Home," and I fell, stricken with anguish, onto the cushion of my car. He had found me and recaptured me.

August 17. What a night! What a night! And yet it feels as if I should rejoice. Until one in the morning, I read. Hermann Herestauss, doctor of philosophy and theogony, has written the history and manifestations of all the invisible beings that prowl around mankind, or that we dream of. He describes their origins, their dwelling-places, their powers. But not one of them resembles the one that is haunting me. We might reason that, ever since man began to think, he has had a premonition and a dread of some new being, stronger than he, his successor in this world, and that, feeling him nearby yet being unable to foresee the nature of this master, he has created, in his terror, the entire fantastic population of occult beings, vague phantoms born from fear.

After reading till one in the morning, I went to sit down near my open window in order to cool my forehead and my thoughts in the calm night breeze.

It was fine and warm out. How I would have loved this night, once upon a time!

No moon. The stars in the depths of the black sky twinkled quaveringly. Who lives in those worlds? What forms, what living beings, what animals, what plants are there? What do the sentient beings in those distant universes know, more than we do? What more are they capable of doing than we? What do they see that we have not the least knowledge of? Some day or other, won't one of them, crossing space, appear on our earth to conquer it, just as long ago the Normans crossed the sea to subjugate people who were weaker?

We are so infirm, so helpless, so ignorant, so small, we others, on this spinning grain of mud mixed with a drop of water.

I dozed off, musing like that, in the cool evening wind.

After sleeping for about forty minutes, though, I reopened my eyes without making a movement, awakened by some confused, strange emotion. At first I saw nothing; then, all of a sudden, it seemed to me that a page of the book that I had left open on my table had just turned, all by itself. No breath of air had entered through my window. I was surprised, and I waited. After about four minutes, I saw, yes, I saw with my own eyes, another page rise up and fall back on the one before, as if a finger had turned it. My armchair was empty, seemed empty; but I understood that he was there, seated in my place, and that he was reading. With a furious leap, the leap of a rebellious animal who is about to disembowel his tamer, I crossed my room to seize him, strangle him, kill him! ...But before I could reach it, my chair was knocked over, as if someone were fleeing before me... my table rocked back and forth, my lamp fell and went out, and my window slammed as if a surprised thief had rushed out into the night, grabbing the shutters.

So he had run away. He had been afraid. He, afraid of me!

Then... then... tomorrow... or the day after... or someday... I'll be able to hold him in my fists, and crush him to the ground! Don't dogs, sometimes, bite and choke their masters?

August 18. I have been thinking all day. Oh, yes, I will obey him, follow his impulses, accomplish all his wishes, make myself humble, submissive, cowardly. He is the stronger one. But a time will come....

August 19. I know... I know... I know everything! I have just read this in the *Revue du Monde Scientifique*:

> *A rather curious piece of news has reached us from Rio de Janeiro. A madness, an epidemic of madness, like the contagious dementias that attacked the population of Europe in the Middle Ages, is raging now in the province of Saõ Paulo. The inhabitants, distraught, are leaving their houses, deserting their villages, abandoning their crops, claiming they are pursued, possessed, ruled like human livestock by invisible but tangible beings, sorts of vampires, which feed on their life while they sleep, and which drink water and milk without seeming to touch any other food.*
>
> *Prof. Dom Pedro Henriquez, accompanied by several learned doctors, has left for the province of Saõ Paulo, in order to study on site the origins and manifestations of this surprising madness, and to suggest to the Emperor the measures he thinks best suited to restore these delirious populations to reason.*

And now I remember it, I remember the fine Brazilian three-master that passed by my windows as it went up the Seine, last May 8th. And I thought it was so pretty, so white, so cheerful! The Being was on it, coming from down there, where his race was born. And he saw me! He saw my white house too; and he jumped from the ship onto the shore. Oh my God!

Now I know, I have guessed. The reign of mankind is over.

He has come, the One the primal terrors of primitive tribes dreaded, the One anxious priests exorcised, the One magicians summoned on dark nights, without ever seeing him appear, the One to whom the premonitions of adepts wandering through the world attributed all the monstrous or gracious forms of gnomes, spirits, genies, fairies, elves. After the coarse imaginings of primitive horror, more perspicacious men had a clearer presentiment of him. Mesmer guessed his existence, and for ten years now doctors have discovered, in an accurate way, the nature of his power before he himself even exercised it. They have played with this weapon of the new Lord, the domination of a mysterious will over a human soul, which turns into a slave. They called it 'magnetism,' 'hypnotism,' 'suggestion'.... What do I know? I have seen them amuse themselves like foolish children with this terrible power. We are cursed. Mankind is cursed. He has come, the... the... what is his name... the... he seems to be shouting out his name to me, and I cannot hear it... the... yes... he is shouting it... I am trying to hear... I can't... again... the... Horla... I heard... the Horla... it is he... the Horla... he has come!

Now the vulture has eaten the dove, the wolf has eaten the lamb; the lion has devoured the sharp-horned buffalo; man has killed the lion with the arrow, with the sword, with powder; but the Horla will make man into what we made the horse and the steer: his thing, his servant and his food, by the simple power of his will. Our woe is upon us.

But the animal sometimes rebels and kills the one who tamed him.... I too want to do this.... I could... but I must recognize him, touch him, see him! Scholars say that the eyes of an animal, different from our own, cannot distinguish objects as our eyes do.... And my eyes cannot distinguish this newcomer who oppresses me.

Why? Now I remember the words of the monk at Mont Saint-Michel: "Do we see the hundred-thou-sandth part of what exists? Look, here is the wind, which is the strongest force in nature, which knocks men down, destroys buildings, uproots trees, whips the sea up into mountains of water, destroys cliffs, and throws great ships onto the shoals; here is the wind that kills, whistles, groans, howls—have you ever seen it, and can you see it? Yet it exists."

And I thought further: My eye is so weak, so imperfect, that I cannot even make out solid objects, if they are transparent as glass! ... If a two-way mirror bars my way, it knocks me down, just as a bird who has flown into a room breaks his neck on the windowpanes. A thousand other things deceive our sight and lead it astray. What is so surprising about our not knowing how to perceive a new body, one that light can pass through?

A new being! Why not? Surely it had to come. Why should we be the last people? If we can't distinguish him, as we can all the other creatures before us, it's because his nature is more perfect, his body finer and more absolute than ours, which is so weak, so clumsily conceived, encumbered with organs that are always weary, always strained, like machinery that is too complex—our body, which lives like a plant, like an animal, feeding with difficulty on air, grass, and meat, an animal machine prey to sicknesses, deformations, putrefactions, short-winded, unstable, simple and strange, naively, poorly made, a coarse and delicate work, a rough outline of a being that could become intelligent and superb.

There are just a few of us in this world, so few species between oysters and men. Why not one more entity, now that the era is over when all the various species appeared in orderly succession?

Why not one more? And why not other trees with immense, dazzling flowers, perfuming entire regions? Why not other elements besides fire, air, earth, and water?—There are four of them, just four, those foster parents of beings! What a pity! Why aren't there forty elements instead, or four hundred, or four thousand? How paltry everything is, how miserly, how wretched! Stingily given, aridly invented, heavily made! Look at the elephant, the hippopotamus—such grace! The camel, such elegance!

But you'll say, what about the butterfly? A flower that flies! I dream of one that would be as large as a hundred universes, with wings whose shape, beauty, color, and movement I cannot even describe. But I can see it... it goes from star to star, refreshing them and soothing them with the harmonious and light breath of its journey!... And the peoples up there, ecstatic and ravished, watch it go by!

. . .

What is wrong with me? It is he, the Horla, who is haunting me, making me think these mad thoughts! He is inside me, he is becoming my soul; I will kill him!

August 19. I will kill him. I have seen him! I had sat down at my table last night, and I pretended to write with great concentration. I was well aware that he would come prowl around me, quite close, so close that I might perhaps be able to touch him, to seize him.... And then... then, I would have the strength of the desperate. I would have my hands, my knees, my chest, my forehead, my teeth to strangle him, crush him, bite him, tear him apart.

And I watched for him with all my overexcited organs.

I had lit both my lamps, along with the eight candles on my mantelpiece, as if, in this brightness, I might expose him.

Opposite me, my bed, an old oaken four-poster; to my right, my fireplace; to my left, my door, which I had carefully shut, after having left it open for a long time, in order to lure him in; behind me, a very high wardrobe with a mirror, which I used every day to shave and dress, and in which I had the habit of looking at myself, from head to foot, every time I passed in front of it.

I was just pretending to write in order to trick him, for he too was spying on me; and suddenly, I felt, I was sure, that he was reading over my shoulder, that he was there, grazing my ear.

I stood up with my hands outstretched, turning around so quickly that I almost fell down. And? Everything there was clear as in full daylight, but I could not see myself in my mirror—it was empty, clear, profound, full of light! My image was not inside it... yet I myself was facing it! I could see the large clear glass from top to bottom. I looked at it with terrified eyes, but dared not move forward. I did not dare to make any movement, fully aware that he was there, but that he would escape me again, he whose imperceptible body had devoured my reflection.

I was terrified. Then suddenly I began to see myself in a mist, in the depths of the mirror, in a mist as if through a sheet of water. It seemed to me that this water shimmered from left to right, slowly, making my image more precise, from second to second. It was like the end of an eclipse. Whatever was obscuring me seemed not to possess any clearly defined outlines, but just a sort of opaque transparency, little by little becoming clearer.

Finally I could distinguish myself completely, just as I do every day when I look at myself.

I had seen him! The terror of it has remained with me, and makes me tremble still.

August 20. How can I kill him, if I cannot touch him? Poison? But he would see me mixing it in the water; and besides, will our poisons even have any effect on an imperceptible body? No... no... they cannot.... What then?

August 21. I have had a locksmith come from Rouen, and ordered iron shutters for my bedroom, the kind certain mansions have in Paris, on the ground floor, because of fear of thieves. He will also make me a door of the same material. I let him think me a coward, but I don't care!

. . .

September 10. Rouen, Hôtel Continental. It is done... it is done... but is he dead? My soul is in turmoil over what I have seen.

Yesterday, after the locksmith had installed my iron shutters and door, I left everything open until midnight, although it was beginning to turn cold.

All of a sudden, I felt that he was there, and a joy, a mad joy seized me. I rose up slowly and paced back and forth, for a long time, so that he wouldn't guess anything was amiss; then I took off my shoes and nonchalantly put on my slippers; then I closed the iron shutters, and, quietly walking to the door, closed it too with a double turn of the lock. Then I came back to the window, locked it with a padlock, and put the key in my pocket.

All of a sudden, I knew that he was getting agitated near me, that it was his turn to be afraid, that he was commanding me to open the window. I almost gave in. I did not give in. Instead, leaning back against the door, I half-opened it, just enough to let me slip through, backwards; since I am very tall, my head touched the lintel. I was certain he had been unable to escape, and I shut him in, all alone, all alone! At last! I had him! Then I ran downstairs. I picked up both the lamps in my drawing-room, which was underneath my bedroom, and poured out all the oil onto the rug, the furniture, everywhere. Then I set fire to it, and ran out, after having carefully closed the large front door with a double turn of the lock.

I ran to the back of my garden to hide in a clump of bay-trees. How long it took! How long it took! Everything was dark, silent, motionless; not a breath of air, not a star, just mountains of clouds that couldn't be seen, but that weighed so heavy, so heavy, on my soul.

I watched my house, and I waited. How long it took! I was beginning to think the fire had put itself out, or that he had put it out, He, when one of the windows on the ground floor caved in under pressure from the fire, and a flame, a huge red and yellow flame, tall, soft, caressing, soared up along the white wall and kissed it all the way up to the roof. A glow ran through the trees, the branches, the leaves, and a shiver, a shiver of fear too! The birds woke up; a dog began to bark; it looked as if dawn were breaking. Immediately two other windows shattered, and I saw that the entire ground floor of my house was nothing more than a terrifying inferno. But a scream, a horrible, high-pitched, penetrating scream, a woman's scream, rent the night, and two garret windows opened. I had forgotten my servants! I saw their terrified faces, and their waving arms.

Then, beside myself with horror, I began to run towards the village, shouting, "Help! Help! Fire! Fire!" I met some people who were already on the way, and I went back with them, to see.

The house, now, was nothing more than a terrible and magnificent pyre, a monstrous pyre, illuminating all the land around, a pyre where people were burning, and where he was burning too, He, He, my prisoner, the new Being, the new master, the Horla!

Suddenly the entire roof caved in between the walls, and a volcano of flames shot up to the sky. Through all the windows opening onto the furnace, I could see the pit of fire, and I thought about him there, in this oven, dead....

—Dead? Maybe not.... What about his body? Wasn't his body, which daylight could go right through, indestructible by all the methods that kill our own bodies?

What if he wasn't dead?... Maybe only time holds sway over that Invisible and Dreadful Being. Why should this body that is transparent, this unknowable body, this Spirit body, have to fear illnesses, wounds, infirmities, premature destruction?

Premature destruction? All the horrors of humanity stem from that alone. After mankind, the Horla. —After our race that can die any day, at any hour, at any minute, from any number of accidents, has come that one, who will only die on his day, at his hour, at his minute, when he has reached the term of his existence!

No... no... of course not... of course he is not dead.... So then—it's me, it's me I have to kill!

. . .

—May 1887

LETTER FROM A MADMAN

FIRST PUBLISHED IN THE FEBRUARY 17, 1885 ISSUE OF THE MAGAZINE GIL BLAS, *UNDER THE PEN NAME "MAUFRIGNEUSE"*

My dear Doctor, I place myself in your hands. Do with me what you like.

I am going to tell you my state of mind very frankly, and you will judge whether it isn't better to have me taken care of for a little while in a sanatorium, rather than leave me prey to the hallucinations and sufferings that are plaguing me.

Here's the story, lengthy and precise, of the singular illness of my soul.

. . .

I was living like everybody else, looking at life with the open, blind eyes of man, without surprise and without understanding. I was living as animals live, as we all live, carrying out all the duties of existence, examining and thinking I saw, thinking I knew, thinking I was familiar with, my surroundings, when one day I perceived that everything is false.

It was a phrase from Montesquieu that suddenly illumined my thinking. Here it is:

"One more organ or one less in our body would give us a different intelligence. In fact, all the established laws as to why our body is a certain way would be different if our body were not that way."

I reflected on that for months on end, and, little by little, a strange clarity came to me, and this clarity let there be night.

In fact, our organs are the only intermediaries between the exterior world and ourselves. That is to say, the inner being, which constitutes *the ego*, is in contact, by means of a few nerve endings, with the exterior being, which constitutes the world.

Beyond the fact that this exterior being escapes us by its size, its lengthy existence, its countless and impenetrable properties, its origins, its future or its aims, its distant forms and its infinite manifestations, our organs provide us only with information as uncertain as it is paltry about the portion of it that we can know.

Uncertain, because it is nothing but the properties of our organs that determine for us the apparent properties of matter.

Paltry, because since our senses number only five, the field of their investigations and the nature of their revelations are both quite limited.

I will explain. The eye transmits dimensions, shapes, and colors to us. It deceives us on these three points.

It can reveal to us only objects and beings of an average dimension in relation to human size, which has led us to apply the word "large" to certain things and the word "small" to certain other things, only because the eye's weakness does not allow it to be aware of what is too immense or too tiny for it. Hence, it knows and sees almost nothing, and almost the entire universe remains hidden from it, the star that inhabits space as well as the microbe that inhabits a drop of water.

Even if our eye had even a hundred million times more than its normal strength, if it perceived in the air that we breathe all the races of invisible beings, and all the inhabitants of neighboring planets, there would still exist an infinite number of races of animals so small, and worlds so distant, that the eye could not see them.

All our ideas about size, then, are false, since there is no limit possible to largeness or to smallness.

Our awareness of dimensions and shapes has no absolute value, since it is determined solely by the power of the organ and in constant comparison with ourselves.

Let us add that the eye is also incapable of seeing the transparent. A flawless glass tricks it. It confuses it with the air, which it does not see either.

Let us move on to color.

Color exists because our eye is constituted in such a way that it transmits to the brain, in the form of color, the various ways that bodies absorb and break down, in accordance with their chemical composition, the light rays that strike them.

The various proportions of this absorption and breaking down make up the shades of color.

Thus this organ imposes on the mind its way of seeing, or rather its arbitrary way of noting dimensions and perceiving the relationships of light with matter.

Let us examine the sense of hearing.

Even more than with the eye, we are the playthings and dupes of this fanciful organ.

Two bodies colliding produce a certain shock in the atmosphere. This movement makes a certain tiny piece of skin vibrate in our ear, which changes immediately into a sound something that is in fact nothing but a vibration.

Nature is silent. But the eardrum possesses the miraculous property of transmitting to us all the quiverings of invisible waves in space in the form of meaning, meaning that changes depending on the number of vibrations.

This metamorphosis, which is performed by the auditory nerve over the short trajectory from the ear to the brain, has allowed us to create a strange art— music—the most poetic and precise of all the arts, vague as a dream and precise as algebra.

What shall we say of the senses of taste and smell? Would we recognize smells and the quality of various foods without the peculiar properties of the nose and the palate?

Humanity, however, could exist without the ear, without taste and smell—that is, without any notion of sound, taste, or smell.

Thus, if we had a few organs less, we would be unaware of admirable and unusual things, but if we had a few organs more, we would discover around us an infinity of other things we would never have suspected while we lacked the means to observe them.

So we deceive ourselves when we pass judgments on the Known. We are surrounded by an unexplored unknown.

Everything is uncertain, and can be perceived in different ways.

Everything is false, everything is possible, everything is doubtful.

Let us formulate this certainty by using the old dictum: "Truth this side of the Pyrénées, error beyond."

And let us say: Truth inside the sense organ, error outside.

Two and two no longer have to make four outside of our atmosphere.

Truth on Earth, error further away. So I conclude that the mysteries we have glimpsed—like electricity, hypnotic sleep, transmission of will, suggestion, all the magnetic phenomena—remain hidden from us, because nature has not provided us with the organ, or organs, necessary to understand them.

After I had convinced myself that everything my senses reveal to me exists only for me as I perceive it, and would be completely different for someone else differently organized, after having concluded that a differently made humanity would have about the world, about life, about everything, ideas that are absolutely opposite to our own, since the consensus of beliefs results only from the similarity of human organs, and differences of opinion come only from slight differences in the functioning of our nerve endings, I made an effort at superhuman thought in order to get some inkling of the impenetrable universe that surrounds me.

Have I gone mad?

I told myself: "I am surrounded by unknown things." I imagined man without ears, suspecting the existence of sound as we suspect so many hidden mysteries, man noting acoustic phenomena whose nature and provenance he cannot determine. And I grew afraid of everything around me—afraid of the air, afraid of the night. From the moment we can know almost nothing, and from the moment that everything is limitless, what remains? Does emptiness actually not exist? What does exist in this apparent emptiness?

And this confused terror of the supernatural, which has haunted mankind since the birth of the world, is legitimate, since the supernatural is nothing other than what remains veiled to us!

Then I understood terror. It seemed to me that I kept brushing against the discovery of a secret of the universe.

I tried to sharpen my organs, to excite them, to make them perceive glimpses of the invisible.

I told myself, "Everything is a being! The shout that passes into the air is an entity like an animal, since it is born, produces a movement, and is again transformed, in order to die. So the fearful mind that believes in incorporeal beings is not wrong. What are they?"

How many men feel them, tremble at their approach, shudder at their imperceptible contact. We feel them around us, but we cannot discern them, for we do not have the eyes to see them, or specifically the unknown organ that could discover them.

Then, more than anyone else, I felt them myself, these supernatural passersby. Beings or mysteries? How can I know? I can't say what they are, but I can always indicate their presence. And I have seen—I have seen an invisible being—as much as one can see them, these beings.

I remained motionless for entire nights, seated in front of my table, my head in my hands, thinking of that, thinking of them. Often I thought an intangible hand, or rather an ungraspable body, was lightly grazing my hair. He didn't touch me, since it wasn't a carnal essence, but an imponderable, unknowable essence.

One evening, I heard the floor creak behind me. It creaked in a strange way. I trembled. I turned around. I saw nothing. And I thought no more of it.

But the next day, at the same time, the same sound occurred. I was so afraid that I got up, certain, certain, certain that I was not alone in my bedroom. I could see nothing. The air was clear, transparent everywhere. My two lamps lit up all corners of the room.

The sound was not repeated, and little by little I calmed down; I remained uneasy, though, and often looked around.

The next day I shut myself in early, looking for a way I could contrive to see the invisible being that was visiting me.

And I saw him. I almost died from the terror of it.

I had lighted all the candles on my mantelpiece and chandelier. The room was illumined as if for a celebration. Both my lamps were burning on my table.

Opposite me, my bed, an old oaken four-poster. To my right, my fireplace. To my left, the door, which I had locked shut. Behind me, a very large wardrobe with a mirror. I looked at myself in it. My eyes looked strange, and my pupils quite dilated.

Then I sat down, as I did every day.

The sound had occurred, the night before and the night before that, at 9:22. I waited. When the precise moment arrived, I perceived an indescribable sensation, as if a fluid, an irresistible fluid, had penetrated me through all the pores of my skin, drowning my soul in an atrocious, true terror. And the creaking sounded, right next to me.

I got up, turning around so quickly that I almost fell down. You could see everything there as if in full daylight, but I couldn't see myself in the mirror! It was empty, clear, full of light. I was not inside it, and yet I was facing it. I looked at it with panic-stricken eyes. I dared not go towards it, since I knew he was between us, he, the invisible one, and he was concealing me.

I was terrified. And then I began to see myself in a mist far back in the mirror, in a mist as if through water; and it seemed to me that this water shimmered left to right, slowly, making me more precise from second to second. It was like the end of an eclipse.

What was hiding me had no outlines, but a kind of opaque transparency that little by little became clearer.

And finally I could see myself clearly, just as I do every day when I look at myself.

I had seen it!

And I did not see it again.

But I wait for it ceaselessly, and I feel that my mind is wandering in this waiting.

I remain for hours, nights, days, weeks, in front of my mirror, waiting for him! He does not come anymore.

He has understood that I've seen him. But I feel that I will wait for him always, until death, that I will wait for him without rest, in front of this mirror, like a hunter lying in wait.

And, in this mirror, I am beginning to see crazy images, monsters, hideous corpses, all kinds of terrifying beasts, atrocious beings, all the unlikely visions that must haunt the minds of madmen.

That is my confession, my dear Doctor. Tell me, what should I do?

. . .

—*February 17, 1885*

THE HORLA

1886

The eminent Dr. Marrande, most renowned of alienists, had asked three of his colleagues and four scholars, who worked in the natural sciences, to come spend an hour at his residence, the sanatorium he directed, to show them one of his patients.

As soon as his friends were assembled, he told them, "I am going to set before you the strangest and most unsettling case I have ever encountered. Moreover, I have nothing to tell you about my client. He will speak for himself." Then the doctor rang. An orderly ushered in a man. He was very thin, as thin as a corpse, as thin as certain madmen who are eaten away by a thought, for a sick thought can devour the body's flesh more than fever or consumption.

When he had greeted everyone and sat down, he started.

Gentlemen, I know why you are gathered here today, and I am ready to tell you my story, just as my friend Dr. Marrande has asked me. For a long time he thought I was mad. Today he is not sure. In a little while, you will all know that I have as healthy, as lucid, as perceptive a mind as your own, unfortunately for me, and for you, and for all of humanity.

But I want to begin with the facts themselves, with the simple facts. Here they are:

I am forty-two years old. I am not married; my wealth is enough to live with a certain luxury. I was living on my estate on the shores of the Seine, in Biessard, near Rouen. I love hunting and fishing. Behind me, beyond the great rocks that tower above my house, I had one of the most beautiful forests in France, the forest of Roumare, and in front of me one of the finest rivers in the world.

My house is immense, painted white on the outside, handsome, ancient, in the middle of a large garden planted with magnificent trees that stretches to the forest, climbing the enormous rocks I just mentioned.

My staff consists, or rather consisted, of a coachman, a gardener, a valet, a cook, and a laundress, who was also a kind of housekeeper. All these people had lived in my home anywhere from ten to sixteen years;

they knew me, knew my house, the countryside, all that surrounded me in my life. They were good, contented servants. That is important for what I am about to tell you.

Let me add that the Seine, which runs alongside my garden, is navigable as far as Rouen, as I'm sure you know. Every day I would see great ships pass by, under sail or steam, coming from all the corners of the world.

A year ago, last Fall, I was suddenly overcome with peculiar and inexplicable feelings of uneasiness. At first it was a sort of nervous anxiety that kept me awake for whole nights at a time. I was so hypersensitive that the least sound made me tremble. My mood turned bitter. I had sudden, inexplicable rages. I called a doctor, who prescribed potassium bromide and showers.

So morning and evening I made myself take showers, and I began to take the bromide. Soon, in fact, I did begin to sleep again, but the sleep was more terrifying than the insomnia. As soon as I went to bed, I closed my eyes and was annihilated. Yes, I fell into the void, into an absolute void, into a death of my entire being from which I was suddenly, horribly jolted by the dreadful feeling of a crushing weight on my chest, and of a mouth that was eating up my life, on my mouth. The shock of it—I've never known anything more horrible.

Imagine to yourselves a man asleep, who has been murdered, and who wakes up with a knife in his throat; and who moans covered with blood, who can no longer breathe, who will die, but who doesn't understand why—that's what it's like.

I kept getting steadily, alarmingly thinner. One day I noticed that my coachman, who had been quite fat, was beginning to grow thin like me.

Finally I asked him:

"What is wrong with you, Jean? You are sick."

He replied:

"I do believe I've caught the same illness as Monsieur. My nights are eating up my days."

I thought at the time that there was a feverish influence in the house because of the proximity of the river, and that I should go away for two or three months, even though we were in the middle of hunting season. But then a small, peculiar fact, observed by chance, brought about such an unlikely, fantastic, and terrifying series of discoveries for me that I stayed home.

I was thirsty one evening, and drank half a glass of water; I noticed that my carafe, standing on the chest of drawers opposite my bed, was full up to the crystal stopper.

During the night, I had one of those dreadful awakenings I've just told you about. I lit my candle, prey to terrible anxiety, and when I went to take another drink of water I saw with astonishment that my carafe was empty. I couldn't believe my eyes.

Either someone had entered my bedroom, or I had become a sleepwalker.

The next evening, I wanted to perform the same test. So I locked my door in order to be sure no one could penetrate my room. I went to sleep and woke up as I did every night. *Someone* had drunk all the water that I had seen two hours before.

Who had drunk this water? Myself, no doubt, and yet I was certain, absolutely certain, that I hadn't made a movement in my deep and painful sleep.

So I resorted to tricks to convince myself that I was not performing these acts unconsciously. One evening I placed, next to the carafe, a bottle of old Bordeaux, a glass of milk (which I hate), and some chocolate cakes (which I love).

The wine and cakes remained intact. The milk and water disappeared. Every day, then, I changed the drinks and the food. Never did *someone* touch the solid, thick foods, and, as to liquids, *someone* drank nothing but fresh milk and above all water.

But this heartbreaking doubt remained in my soul. Couldn't I be the one who was getting up without being aware of it, and who was drinking even the things I disliked, since my senses, numbed by somnambulistic sleep, might be changed, might have lost their ordinary dislikes and acquired different tastes?

So I used a new trick against myself. I wrapped strips of white muslin on all the objects that would certainly have to be touched, and I covered them all with a cotton napkin.

Then, when it was time for me to go to bed, I smeared my hands, lips, and moustache with graphite.

When I woke up, all the objects remained spotless, although someone had touched them, for the napkin was not placed as I had left it; and, moreover, someone had drunk the water and the milk. Yet my door, which I had shut with a safety lock, and my shutters, padlocked as a precaution, would have kept anyone out of the room.

Then I asked myself the overwhelming question: Who was there, every night, close to me?

I sense, gentlemen, that I am telling you all of this too quickly. You are smiling, your opinion has already been formed: "He is a madman." I should have described to you at length my emotions, the emotions of a man who, locked up at home, with a healthy mind, sees, through the glass of a carafe, a little water that has vanished while he slept. I should have made you understand this torture renewed every night and every morning, and that invincible sleep, and those even more dreadful awakenings.

But I will go on.

All of a sudden, the miracle stopped. *Someone* no longer touched anything in my room. It was over. I was feeling better. My happiness returned, when I learned that one of my neighbors, Monsieur Legite, was in just the same condition that I had been in myself. I believed again in a feverish influence in the countryside. My coachman had left me a month ago, very ill.

The winter passed, and spring began. One morning, as I was walking near my rose garden, I saw, I distinctly saw, quite close to me, the stem of one of the most beautiful roses break as if an invisible hand had picked it. Then the flower followed the curve an arm would have described as it carried it to a mouth, where it remained suspended in the transparent air, all alone, motionless, terrifying, three feet from my eyes.

Seized with mad horror, I hurled myself on it to seize it. I found nothing. It had disappeared. Then I was overcome with a furious rage against myself. A reasonable and serious man cannot permit himself such hallucinations!

But was it indeed a hallucination? I looked for the stem. I found it immediately on the bush, freshly broken, between two other roses that had remained on the branch; for there had been three of them, as I had seen perfectly.

I returned home, my soul in turmoil. Gentlemen, listen to me, I am calm; I did not believe in the supernatural, I do not even believe in it today; but, from that moment onward, I was sure, sure as I am of day and night, that there existed near me an invisible being who had haunted me, then left me, and who was returning.

A little later I had proof of this.

Among my servants every day furious arguments broke out for a hundred reasons that seemed trivial at first, but soon were full of meaning for me.

A glass, a beautiful Venetian glass, broke all by itself, on the hutch in my dining room, in the middle of the day.

The valet accused the cook, who accused the laundress, who accused I don't know who.

Doors that had been closed at night were open in the morning. Someone was stealing the milk every night from the pantry.

What was it? What was its nature? A nervous curiosity, mixed with anger and horror, kept me day and night in a state of constant agitation.

But the house grew calm once again. I was beginning to believe it was all a dream, when the following happened:

It was July 20th, at nine o'clock in the evening. It was very hot out; I had left my window wide open, my lamp lit on my table, illuminating a volume of Musset's poems opened to his "May Night"; I had stretched out in a big armchair and fallen asleep.

I slept for about forty minutes, then opened my eyes, without making any movement, awakened by some strange, confused emotion. At first I saw nothing, then all of a sudden it seemed to me that a page of the book had just turned all by itself. No breath of air had come in through the window. I was surprised and I waited. After about four minutes, I saw, I saw, yes, I saw, gentlemen, with my own eyes, another page lift itself and fall back on the preceding one as if a finger had turned it. The chair seemed empty, but I realized that it was there, *it*! I crossed my room in a single bound to seize it, to touch it, to grasp it, if that were possible... But the chair, before I could reach it, toppled over as if someone were fleeing from me; my lamp too fell and went out, the glass broken; and my window was slammed as if an some thief had seized it as he fled, striking at the latch...

I threw myself at the bell-pull and called out. When my valet appeared, I said to him:

"I've knocked everything over and broken everything. Give me some light."

I slept no more that night. But I thought I might once again have been the plaything of an illusion. When one wakes up, one's senses are still confused. Wasn't it I who had knocked over my chair and my light, hurrying like a madman?

No, it was not me! I knew it so positively I didn't doubt it for a second. And yet I wanted to believe it was me.

Wait. The Being. What should I call him? The Invisible. No, that's not good enough. I baptized him the Horla. Why? I have no idea. The Horla, then, scarcely ever left me. Day and night I had the sensation, the certainty, of the presence of this elusive neighbor, and I was certain too that he was taking my life, hour by hour, minute by minute.

The impossibility of seeing him exasperated me, so I kept all the lamps lit in my rooms, as if I could reveal him with all this brightness.

I saw him, finally.

You do not believe me. But I did see him. I was sitting in front of some book, not reading, but keeping watch, with all my overexcited senses, keeping watch for the one I felt so close to me. He was definitely there. But where? What was he doing? How could I reach him?

Across from me was my bed, an old oaken four-poster. To my right, the fireplace. To my left, the door, which I had carefully closed. Behind me, a very large wardrobe with a mirror I used every day to shave and get dressed, and in which I had the habit of looking at myself from head to foot every time I passed in front of it.

So I was pretending to read, in order to trick him, for he too was spying on me; and suddenly I felt, I was certain that he was reading over my shoulder, that he was there, grazing my ear.

I stood up, turning around so quickly that I almost fell over. You could see everything in the room as if in full daylight... but I did not see myself in my mirror! It was empty, clear, full of light. My image was not inside it.... Yet I was facing it.... I saw the large glass, limpid from top to bottom! I watched it with panic-stricken eyes, and I no longer dared to move forward, feeling him between us, him, aware that he would escape me again, but that his imperceptible body had absorbed my reflection.

I was terrified. Then suddenly I began to see myself in a mist in the depths of the mirror, in a mist as if through a sheet of water; and it seemed to me that this water shimmered from left to right, slowly, making my image more precise from second to second. It was just like the end of an eclipse. What was hiding me did not seem to possess clearly defined outlines, but a sort of opaque transparency that little by little grew clearer.

Finally I was able to distinguish myself completely, just as I do every day when I look at myself.

I had seen him. The horror of it has remained with me, and makes me shudder still.

The next day I was here, where I begged them to keep me.

Now, gentlemen, I will conclude.

Dr. Marrande, after doubting me for a long time, finally decided to travel alone to my country.

"Three of my neighbors are currently affected just as I was. Isn't that true?"

The doctor replied, "It's true."

"You advised them to leave out some water and milk every night in their bedroom to see if these liquids would disappear. Did these liquids disappear, as they did at my house?"

The doctor replied with a solemn gravity, "They disappeared."

So, gentlemen, a Being, a new Being, who no doubt will soon multiply just as we have multiplied, has just appeared on Earth.

Ah! You smile! Why? Because this Being remains invisible. But our eye, gentlemen, is such an elementary organ that it can scarcely discern what is indispensable to our existence. Whatever is too small escapes it, whatever is too large escapes it, whatever is too far away escapes it. It is unaware of the animals that live in a drop of water. It is unaware of the inhabitants, the plants, and the surface of neighboring stars; it can't even see what is transparent.

Place in front of it a perfect two-way mirror, and it will not perceive it, it will make us walk right into it, just as a bird caught in a house breaks his neck on the windowpanes. It does not see the solid and transparent bodies that nevertheless exist; it does not see the air we live on, does not see the wind that is the strongest force in nature, that knocks men down, topples buildings, uproots trees, whips the sea up into mountains of water that make granite cliffs crumble.

Why should it be surprising if our eye cannot see a new body, one that evidently lacks the property of blocking light rays?

Can you see electricity? And yet it exists!

This being, which I have named the Horla, also exists.

Who is it? Gentlemen, it is the one the Earth is waiting for, the one that will succeed mankind! The one who is coming to dethrone us, subjugate us, tame us, feed on us perhaps, just as we fed on the ox and the wild boar.

For centuries, we have had a foreboding of him, we have dreaded him and foretold him! The fear of the Invisible always haunted our ancestors.

He has come.

All the fairy tales, the legends about goblins and ungraspable and malevolent prowlers of the air, it was he they were talking about, he is the one of whom an already anxious and trembling humanity had some premonition.

And everything you yourselves have been doing, gentlemen, in recent years, what you call 'hypnotism,' 'suggestion,' 'magnetism'—it is he you are heralding and prophesying!

I tell you he has come. He prowls about, anxious himself as the first men were, still ignorant of his own force and power that he will come to know soon, too soon.

And now, gentlemen, to finish, a fragment from a newspaper I came across, which comes from Rio de Janeiro. I quote:

> *A sort of epidemic of madness seems for some time to have been raging in the province of Saõ Paulo. The inhabitants of several villages have run away, abandoning their land and their houses, claiming they are pursued and consumed by invisible vampires that are feeding on their breath while they sleep and that otherwise drink nothing but water, and sometimes milk!*

I will add: A few days before the first attack of the sickness from which I almost died, I vividly recall seeing a grand Brazilian three-master pass by with its flag flying... I told you that my house was on the water's edge... all white.... He was hidden on this ship, without a doubt....

I have nothing more to add, gentlemen.

Dr. Marrande rose and murmured:

"Nor I. I do not know if this man is mad, or if we are both mad... or if... if our successor has actually arrived."

. . .

The word "horla" (pronounced "orla"), although not a word in French, does have some interesting connotations to a French ear. "*Hors*" means outside, and "*là*" means simply "there"—so *le* (note the masculine gender) *Horla* sounds like the Outsider, the outer, the one Out There.

Maupassant seems to have been much taken with the Horla, since he wrote two versions of the story, in 1886 and 1887, as well as the more austere, but no less frightening "Letter from a Madman" (1885). All three are included here, in a new, integral presentation of the Horla cycle.

Maupassant also wrote a short story called "The Voyage of The Horla," which was published in July 1887, just a few months after the final version of "The Horla." "The Voyage of the Horla" does not, however, deal with the supernatural: It is about a journey in a hot-air balloon called "Le Horla," about how interesting the earth looks when viewed from far away, from Out There.

CHARLOTTE MANDELL
ANNANDALE-ON-HUDSON, NY
DECEMBER 2004

THE ART OF THE NOVELLA SERIES

THE CONTEMPORARY ART OF THE NOVELLA SERIES